# The Little Bit SCARY People

Boo!
Jules!

# The Little Bit SCARY People

WRITTEN BY Emily Jenkins

ILLUSTRATED BY Alexandra Boiger

HYPERION BOOKS FOR CHILDREN · NEW YORK

AN IMPRINT OF DISNEY BOOK GROUP

The big boy with thick eyebrows rides his skateboard on the sidewalk and cranks the radio so loud, my dad yells out the window for him to turn it down.

He's a little bit SCARY.

But I bet,
when he wakes up in the morning,
he kisses his cat on the head and scratches
her neck until she purrs.

The bus driver won't let me on if I don't have the right change. She honks her horn loudly, when she doesn't even need to.

She's a little bit SCARY.

But I bet
she makes fancy breakfasts in the morning for her kids:
pancakes, waffles, or English muffins with eggs and chopped tomato.

The principal of my school has long, shiny fingernails, and if she sees me in the hall, she asks if I have a pass.

She's a little bit SCARY.

But I bet,
after school on Thursdays,
she takes dancing lessons with her boyfriend
and really, really, shakes it loose.

The music teacher tells the kids to "zip it!"
and picks on me when I can't sing in tune.

He's a little bit SCARY.

But I bet,
late in the evenings,
he reads cowboy stories on the couch, with a big
shaggy dog for company.

The cafeteria lady wears strange rubber gloves and never lets anyone take more than one milk.

She's a little bit SCARY.

But I bet,
when school gets out,
she goes for a jog, listening to show tunes on her headphones.
She sings as loud as she can and doesn't care if people hear.

The school nurse wipes my scraped knee with orange lotion that stings
and tells me he once knew a kid who broke an ankle jumping off a swing like that.

He's a little bit SCARY.

But I bet,
when he gets home from work,
his children pile on his lap and pull on his
ears while he plays them songs on the piano.

The girl in my science class eats bits
of her pencil and mutters to herself
as if no one was listening.

She's a little bit SCARY.

But I bet
she is learning to ride a bicycle after school. She has a red two-wheeler
with a banana seat and streamers on the handles, and her mom runs alongside,
in case she loses her balance.

Outside the candy store, the teenage girl in a leather coat kicks the trash can—just to hear the racket it makes.

She's a little bit SCARY.

But I know,
before dinner,
she plays football with her little brothers and always lets them win.

I know. Because she's my sister.

The policeman on the corner near our house blows his whistle very loud and scolds people for jaywalking.

He's a little bit SCARY.

But I know,
on Friday evenings,
he and his wife and kids go eat
spaghetti at their favorite restaurant.
He likes the garlic bread but worries
about his breath.

I know.
Because he's my dad.

Some people are a little bit SCARY.

But then,
sometimes
(most times, maybe, I think)
sometimes

they really are not.

*To my students in the New York University Gallatin School "Writing for Children" course,*
*without whom this book would never have been good enough*
—E.J.

*To Tatiana and Luis, my not so scary friends*
—A.B.

Text copyright © 2008 by Emily Jenkins · Illustrations copyright © 2008 by Alexandra Boiger

For information address Hyperion Books for Children, 114 Fifth Avenue, New York, New York 10011-5690.
First Edition · 1 3 5 7 9 10 8 6 4 2 · This book is set in Futura Light · Designed by Elizabeth H. Clark · Printed in Singapore · Reinforced binding · Library of Congress Cataloging-in-Publication Data on file. · ISBN 978-1-4231-0075-1 · Visit www.hyperionbooksforchildren.com